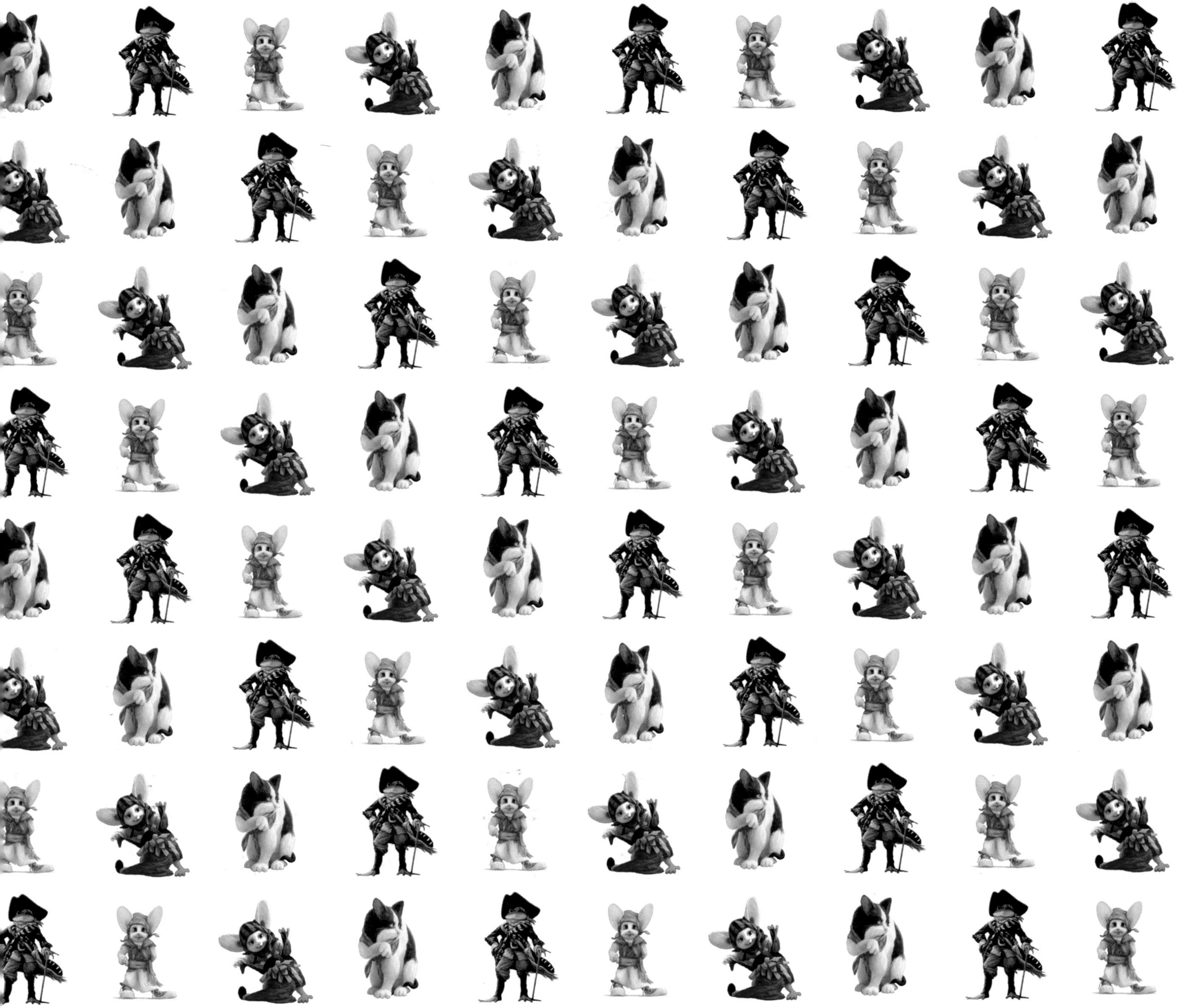

To Pattie, Elias, Noe, Melissa, and Rafael

PUBLISHED BY RIP SQUEAK PRESS
AN IMPRINT OF RIP SQUEAK, INC.
23 SOUTH TASSAJARA DRIVE
SAN LUIS OBISPO, CALIFORNIA 93405

RIP SQUEAK®, JESSE & BUNNY™, ABBEY™, EURIPIDES™, and
RIP SQUEAK AND HIS FRIENDS™ are trademarks of Rip Squeak, Inc.

Library of Congress Control Number: 2004098078

ISBN 0-9672422-9-0
Printed in China by Phoenix Asia
1 3 5 7 9 10 8 6 4 2

Edited and designed by Cheshire Studio
Special thanks to Lois Sarkisian and Jack Rea

Don't miss the other books in this series:
RIP SQUEAK AND HIS FRIENDS *and* THE TREASURE

*To learn more about Rip Squeak and
the art of Leonard Filgate visit*
RipSqueak.com

RIP SQUEAK AND FRIENDS
The Adventure

Written by **Susan Yost-Filgate**

Illustrated by **Leonard Filgate**

RIP SQUEAK PRESS ～ SAN LUIS OBISPO, CALIFORNIA

RIP SQUEAK AND HIS FRIENDS were setting off on their first trip aboard *Adventure,* the sailing ship they found on the pond near the house where they lived.

Aboard were Rip Squeak the mouse, his sister Jesse and her doll, Bunny, and their new friends, Abbey the kitten and Euripides the frog.

As a gentle breeze carried them away from shore, a thick fog engulfed the little vessel and her crew.

The fog made everything look spooky.

"This will ruin our adventure," said Rip.

"Don't be so quick to judge, my salty friend!" said Euripides. "One can never really know when one will find adventure."

As they settled in to wait for the fog to lift, they heard a rumbling sound coming from across the pond.

The sound got louder and louder, like thunder on a rainy day. The still water of the pond started to ripple with waves, which caused the ship to heave up and down as if something were pushing it from below.

"Looks like we'll have an adventure after all!" shouted Rip, as he grabbed a rope that hung from the mast.

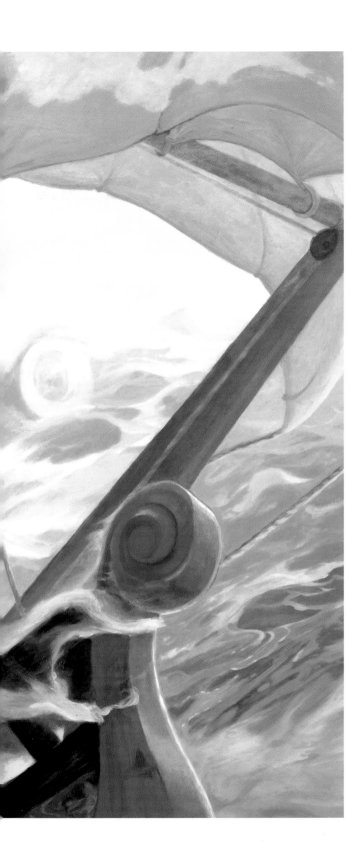

Rip clung to the rope and looked out over the water to see what was going on. That's when the head of a gigantic odd creature rose out of the swirling waves.

Everyone shrieked when they saw the scary face.

"A monster!" yelled Abbey as she wrapped her paws around Jesse to protect her.

Suddenly, as quickly as it had appeared, the creature vanished.

Within seconds, the pond was calm again.

"What was that?" Jesse squealed, clutching Bunny closely.

"I think it must have been a pond monster!" Euripides proclaimed.

"A p-p-pond monster?" Abbey stuttered, a bit shaken. "But that's impossible! There's no such thing as a pond monster."

Rip climbed back up the rope to get a better view. "I don't see any monsters," he said. "There's nothing out there but water."

"Rip!" Jesse shouted as the water started to roll once again. "Hold on!"

When the ship rocked back and forth Rip lost his grip and was tossed over the side.

"Oh no!" yelled Jesse as she watched her brother disappear into the thick, gray fog and rolling waves.

What no one on board the little ship could see was that Rip had landed right on the pond monster's back!
The startled creature bolted through the waves like a speedboat, with Rip clutching tightly as the water splashed all around him.

With an unexpected jolt, the creature dropped Rip like a
waterlogged towel onto soft, dry sand at the edge of the pond.
He was safe! Had the monster really saved him?
Rip rubbed the water from his eyes and sat up.

The monster was right in front of him, hissing and snarling.

"You don't scare me!" said Rip, as he looked directly at the creature. "You saved me, so you can't be a *real* monster."

The startled creature began to cry. A big tear dripped off its snout and splashed in the sand.

"I don't scare you?" the creature sniveled. "But I *look* like a monster. I have huge eyeballs, sharp claws, and I'm slimy. What else can I be?"

"Well," Rip replied, "you can be anything you want to be. My friend Abbey is a cat, but she doesn't try to eat mice like most cats, because that's not what's in her heart. You might look like a monster, but I don't think you really are one. You just like to pretend."

"What does that mean?" asked the creature.

"It's what my friend Euripides does," Rip told him. "He's an actor. An actor pretends to be something he isn't. Why, right now, he's pretending to be a pirate captain. I think you're pretending to be a scary monster."

The creature smiled and said, "You're right. I don't really feel like a monster."

"Let's go back to the ship," suggested Rip. "I'll introduce you to my friends. But you must promise not to be too scary this time."

"Okay," the monster giggled, "and I'll try not to make waves, too."

"My name's Rip, what's yours?"

"I'm Salvador," said the creature. "Hop on."

Salvador swam so gently, he didn't make a single ripple in the pond. In fact, he was so quiet Euripides, Abbey, and Jesse jumped when he suddenly peered over the side of the ship and very politely said, "Excuse me, I think I have something you lost." Then he raised his tail and Rip casually slid down onto the deck.

"Hi, everybody!" exclaimed Rip, grinning happily.
"Rip!" everyone shouted gleefully. "Are we glad to see you!"
Abbey and Jesse hugged him so tightly he squeaked.

"We have a new friend," Rip announced. "This is Salvador. He saved my life when I fell overboard. He was just pretending to be a scary monster."

"Well, I found him *quite* convincing," said Euripides. "Congratulations on an outstanding performance, old boy! You must be an actor at heart."

Salvador beamed and took a little bow.

"The fog is beginning to lift," said Euripides. "It's time we turned this ship toward shore."

"Can we see you again tomorrow, Salvador?" asked Rip.

"I'll be here—pretending," he replied, making a scary monster face. "How was that?"

"*Most* realistic," said Euripides, waving good-bye.

"I guess the fog didn't ruin our adventure after all," Jesse said to Rip.

"You're right," he said, putting his arm around his sister. "It turned out to be an amazing day. We made another new friend and we had a great adventure."

"Let's come about and head for shore," Euripides said, standing by Rip, as the little mouse took the helm and steered the ship toward home.